Home-Alone Kids

Katacha Díaz

Rigby

During the school year, millions of kids across the United States leave their classrooms between 2:00 and 3:30 in the afternoon. Some of these children go home to a waiting parent, but with more parents working, many kids spend their afternoons at a day-care center, or being cared for by relatives, friends, neighbors, housekeepers, or sitters. Still more kids come home to an empty house and spend their afternoons caring for themselves.

What do home-alone kids do between the time they get home from school and the time their parents get home from work? And how would they handle an emergency situation?

This book presents a variety of situations based on interviews and information gathered from real kids. It also provides basic safety tips for home-alone kids. We encourage kids to share their feelings and concerns about being home alone with their parents, and work out solutions together.

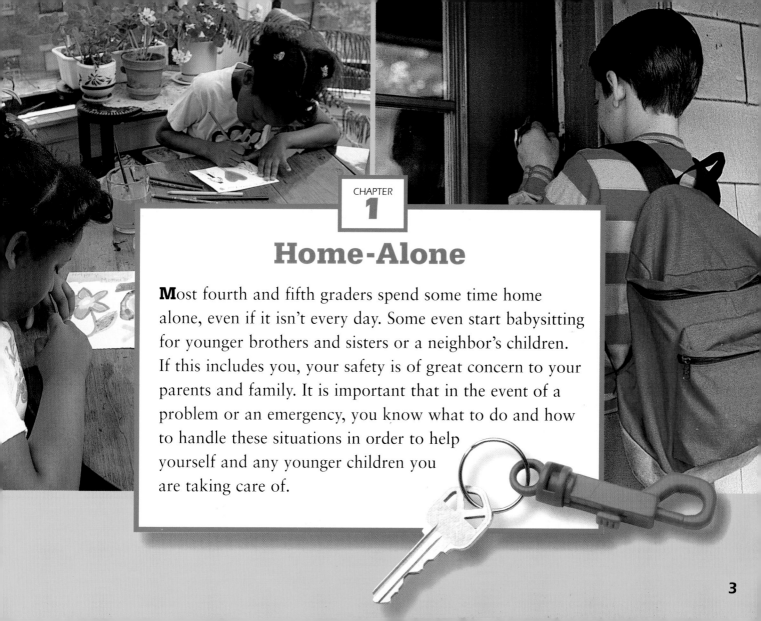

Home-Alone

Most fourth and fifth graders spend some time home alone, even if it isn't every day. Some even start babysitting for younger brothers and sisters or a neighbor's children. If this includes you, your safety is of great concern to your parents and family. It is important that in the event of a problem or an emergency, you know what to do and how to handle these situations in order to help yourself and any younger children you are taking care of.

David is nine years old, and a fourth-grade student at a public elementary school. He is an only child. Both his father and mother leave for work very early. David spends about an hour each morning and two-and-a-half hours each afternoon at home alone.

David's mom wakes him up every morning before she leaves for work. His parents leave a message for him each morning, taped on the refrigerator, that David reads before going to school. This system works well for David and his parents.

Hi David,

1. Don't forget your house key.

2. Lock the front door.

3. Call Mom as soon as you get home from school. If Mom is in a meeting, she'll call you back as soon as she can.

4. No friends allowed in the house.

5. Check the list for today's chore.

Love you!
Mom and Dad

Every day when David gets home from school, he looks around the outside of his house, just like his parents taught him to do. If there were an open door or broken window, David would not go in. Instead, he would go to a neighbor's house to call the police and one of his parents. Luckily this has never happened, but it is good to be careful.

Each day David calls his mom at work to let her know that he's arrived home safely. He has a bowl of his favorite energy snack mix or fixes chocolate pudding (see David's recipes, right), and works on his homework.

CHOCOLATE PUDDING MIX

MILK

David's Energy Mix

1 cup of granola cereal
1 cup of chocolate chips
1 cup of peanuts
1 cup of sunflower seeds
1 cup of raisins
1 cup of dried cranberries
Combine in large mixing bowl.
Store in plastic container with a
tight-fitting lid. (6 cups)

Chocolate Pudding

2 tablespoons instant chocolate pudding mix
1/3 cup cold milk
Mix instant chocolate pudding and cold milk
in a cup. Stir until thick. (1 serving)

After he finishes his homework, David does his daily chore and marks off on the list that the chore is done. Sometimes he watches television, but for the most part, David plays computer games until his mom arrives home at 5:00. His dad usually gets home around 6:30. Shortly afterward, David and his parents sit down to have dinner together and talk about the events of their day.

David's List of Chores

	M	T	W	Th	F
Load dishwasher (Monday)	√				
Set the table (Tuesday)		√			
Collect newspapers and put in recycling bin (Wednesday)			√		
Clean your room (Thursday)				√	
Day off! (Friday)					
Collect allowance on Saturday!					

Home-Alone House Rules

Staying home alone is a joint responsibility between parents and their kids, so it's important to plan a family meeting to discuss and establish house rules for you when you are alone. It's a good idea to have rules regarding using the telephone, answering the telephone and front door, doing homework, watching television, using the computer and kitchen appliances, making snacks, playing outside, having friends over, chores, and whatever else you and your parents come up with. Write the house rules down, post them, and review them regularly at family meetings. This will avoid misunderstandings.

Call Mom after school.

Sarah is ten years old and in fourth grade. Her sister Jenny is six years old and in first grade. Both girls attend a private elementary school in their neighborhood. The girls' parents are divorced. They live with their mom during the week, and spend weekends with their dad and stepmother. Sarah and Jenny walk to and from school together, and are home alone in their apartment for an hour-and-a-half each day.

The girls and their mom had a family meeting to talk about and establish home-alone house rules and responsibilities. Since Sarah is the oldest, she's in charge of Jenny. She's also responsible for enforcing the rules, reporting problems, and responding to emergencies.

Sarah and Jenny's home-alone rules and instructions are posted on a bulletin board in the kitchen.

Sarah and Jenny's Rules and Instructions

Care of Jenny:
✔ Sarah is in charge.
✔ Sarah is to call Mom and report any problems with Jenny.

Phone calls:
✔ Call Mom when we get home.
✔ Mom will call us with a secret ring. Wait for the secret ring before we answer the phone. Otherwise we should not answer the phone. Let the answering machine take a message.
✔ Call 911 in case of an emergency. Call Mom, the next-door neighbor, or a friend if it's not an emergency but we need help.
✔ We can each call friends after school, but calls cannot be longer than 15 minutes.

Strangers:
✔ Do not answer the door.
✔ Front door must be locked at all times.
✔ If someone tries to come into the apartment, call 911.

Play rules:
✔ Stay inside the apartment.
✔ No friends are allowed to come over when Mom's not home.

Cooking rules:
✔ Do not use the stove.
✔ Sarah may use the microwave to fix popcorn or heat up leftovers for a snack.

Being Prepared

It's a good idea to have a list of rules and instructions like Sarah and Jenny do. It's also wise to discuss what should be done in different kinds of emergencies.

For example, one day the power went out, but Sarah and Jenny knew what to do because they had planned for such a possibility with their mom. Sarah got out the flashlight that they keep in the kitchen. Each of the girls also has a flashlight in her bedroom she can use. Then Sarah called their mom at work to let her know there had been a blackout. Her mom called the electric company to find out how long the power would be out, and then let the girls know. Sarah and Jenny did not panic. While they waited for the power to be restored, they told jokes and had a milk-and-cookies picnic in the dark!

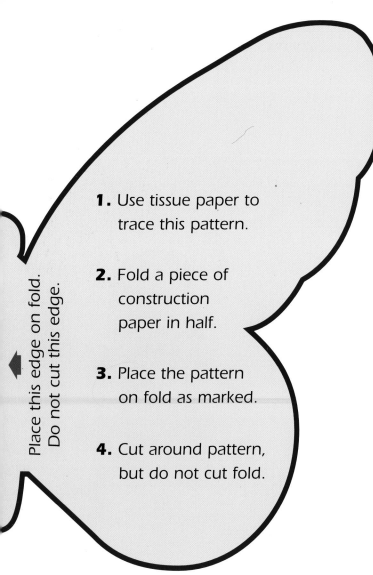

1. Use tissue paper to trace this pattern.

2. Fold a piece of construction paper in half.

3. Place the pattern on fold as marked.

4. Cut around pattern, but do not cut fold.

One of the girls' favorite activities is to work on arts-and-crafts projects after they get home from school—especially on Friday afternoons when Sarah has free time and can help Jenny.

Sarah and Jenny's Butterfly Kites

You will need:
- ✔ tissue paper
- ✔ construction paper in different colors
- ✔ scissors
- ✔ crayons or paints
- ✔ crepe paper, ribbons, or yarn
- ✔ stapler
- ✔ string

1. To make a butterfly pattern, follow the instructions at left.

2. Use the pattern to draw butterflies on different colored sheets of construction paper, and cut them out.

3. Paint designs on each butterfly for decoration.

4. To connect the butterflies to each other, staple the top wing of one butterfly to the bottom wing of the other butterfly.

5. Use crepe paper, ribbons, or yarn to make streamers, and staple to each wing.

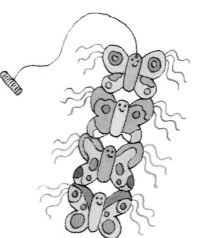

6. Cut a small hole on the head of the top butterfly and attach a piece of string to the top of the kite. Have fun flying it outdoors!

Sarah and Jenny's Tissue Paper Flowers

You will need:
✔ tissue paper in different bright colors
✔ colored pipe cleaners
✔ scissors
✔ pencil

1. Outline the top of a medium-sized bowl on four pieces of brightly colored tissue paper. Cut out the circles.

2. Lay the four pieces on top of each other.

3. Gather tissue paper together in the center, like a bow tie.

4. Take colored pipe cleaner and wrap tightly around the center of the tissue paper.

5. Gently pull each layer apart to make the flower.

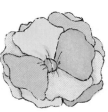

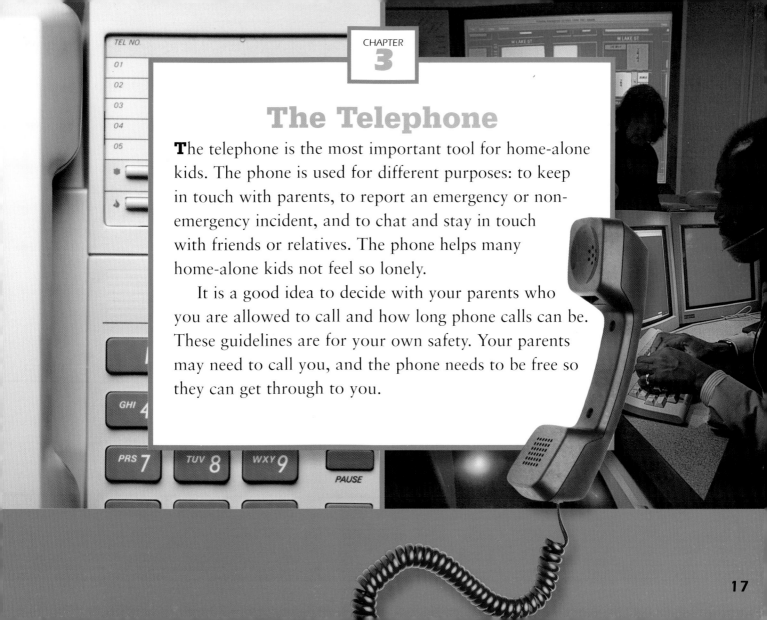

The Telephone

The telephone is the most important tool for home-alone kids. The phone is used for different purposes: to keep in touch with parents, to report an emergency or non-emergency incident, and to chat and stay in touch with friends or relatives. The phone helps many home-alone kids not feel so lonely.

It is a good idea to decide with your parents who you are allowed to call and how long phone calls can be. These guidelines are for your own safety. Your parents may need to call you, and the phone needs to be free so they can get through to you.

Victoria is nine years old, in fourth grade, and is an only child. Victoria's mother died several years ago, and she lives with her dad. Victoria spends two hours each day after school home alone.

Victoria and her dad agreed that she could call her friends after school, but that no call should last longer than 15 minutes. Her dad also taught Victoria how to answer

the phone when she is home alone. For example, if someone calls and asks, "Who is this?" or "What number is this?", Victoria is never to give the caller her name or phone number. Instead, she asks, "Who are you calling?" or "What number are you calling?" Then she tells the caller he or she has the wrong number and hangs up.

If someone calls for her dad, Victoria is never to tell the caller that her dad isn't home and that she is home alone. Instead, Victoria says, "My dad is busy and can't come to the phone right now. May I take a message and have him call you back?"

Also, if someone makes a threatening call, Victoria's dad told her to say nothing and hang up immediately, then to call him at work. Victoria's phone has caller ID, so the caller's name and telephone number is usually displayed on the screen. This

information and the time and date of the call is stored. Victoria's dad can get it and use it to report the incident to the police and/or telephone company.

Victoria and her dad practiced these phone call situations. Her dad pretended to be a stranger and called Victoria so that she could practice saying what he taught her. Now Victoria feels comfortable answering the phone when she's home alone and knows what to tell the caller.

Emergency Phone Numbers

It's also very important to have a list of emergency phone numbers and to keep the list by your phone. If you have more than one phone at home, it's a good idea to have a copy of the list taped by each phone. Review the list of emergency phone numbers at family meetings and keep it up-to-date.

Rob is ten years old, and in the fourth grade. Rob has an older sister, Katy, who is sixteen and a junior in high school. Katy, however, is involved in several after-school activities, so she's not available to care for her younger brother. Rob must care for himself for an hour-and-a-half until his mom arrives home at 5:00. When Rob gets home from school, he is allowed to go outside to play and walk his dog in the neighborhood.

Rob and Katy sat down with their parents to make a list of emergency phone numbers. They typed the list on the family's computer and printed copies for each phone in their house. Since the list is on the computer, it is easy to update and print revised copies.

Emergency Phone Number List

Family Names: (list first and last names)

Home Address: (home address and the
    nearest cross street)

Home Phone Number: (include area code)

Burglar alarm code:

Mom's Work Number:

Mom's Cell Phone Number:

Dad's Work Number:

Dad's Cell Phone Number:

Police Department: **911** or local number

Fire Department: **911** or local number

Emergency Medical Services: **911** or
    local number

Doctor's Name:

Doctor's Phone Number:

Poison Control Center:

Neighbor:

Neighbor:

Relative:

Friend:

Friend:

Emergency Calls

In the event of an emergency, it's really important to stay calm and not to panic, and go to the phone and dial three numbers—**9-1-1**. This is a central emergency number that routes calls to the police and fire departments. The person who answers your **911** emergency call is called the *dispatcher*. The dispatcher will ask you some questions to make sure they send the right kind of emergency help as quickly as possible.

The four **W**'s of **911** are:

✔ **Who** you are (first and last names)

✔ **Where** you are (address and nearest cross street)

✔ **What** happened (describe type of emergency)

✔ **Wait** until the dispatcher tells you to hang up the telephone.

Again, always remember to stay calm and speak quickly and clearly. Give the dispatcher your name, home address and nearest cross street, phone number, and tell them what happened or what is happening. Do not hang up the phone until the dispatcher tells you to. The dispatcher, for example, may give you instructions on what to do or tell you to leave your house immediately. It is very important for you to follow the dispatcher's instructions, and do exactly what they tell you to do. It could save your life and that of others as well.

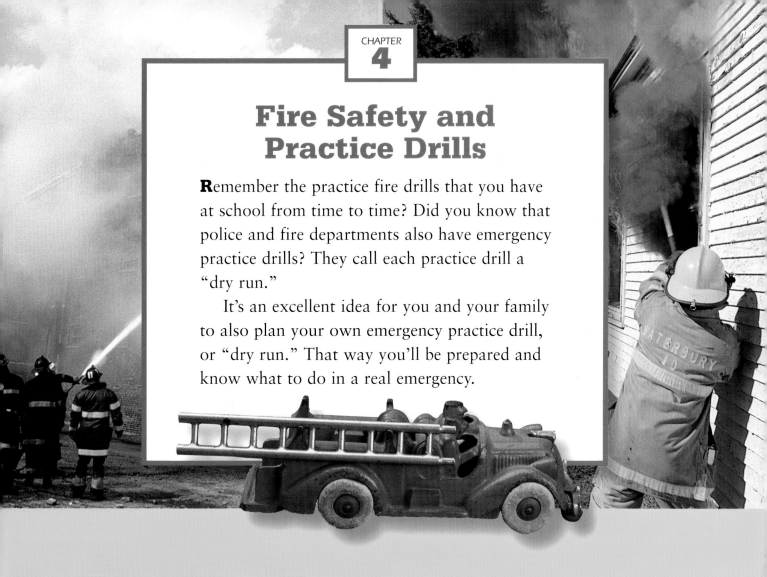

Fire Safety and Practice Drills

Remember the practice fire drills that you have at school from time to time? Did you know that police and fire departments also have emergency practice drills? They call each practice drill a "dry run."

It's an excellent idea for you and your family to also plan your own emergency practice drill, or "dry run." That way you'll be prepared and know what to do in a real emergency.

If you hear a smoke or fire alarm or discover a fire or see smoke at home, there are three important rules to always remember. They are:

1. **Leave your house or apartment immediately!**
   If you have brothers, sisters, or friends at home, try to get them out immediately with you. Leave your front door unlocked, but closed, so the firemen can get in easily. Don't go back inside to get your favorite toys. Toys and things can be replaced. Wait until the firemen tell you that it's safe to go back inside your home.

2. **Go to a neighbor's house and call the fire department.** Remember the four W's of 911, and try to stay calm, speak clearly, and provide the dispatcher with the necessary information.

   If you live in an apartment, learn the location of the nearest fire alarm box and how to use it.

3. **Then call your parents.**

To be prepared for various emergencies, make a list of situations, such as a fire, accident, power outage, gas leak, flood, funny noises, strangers on your property, and any others you can think of. Next, write down what you would say when placing an emergency call. Afterward, practice saying it with your parents and family, even if you feel silly at first. Check your emergency phone numbers list and practice making the call.

My name is _____. I have an emergency.

There is a _____ _____.

My address is _____

and the cross street is _____.

My phone number is _____.

Also, practice your plan of action. Rob's family got together to go over their fire-escape plan. They identified two ways out of every room, and every possible exit from their home, including windows. They also decided where they would meet outside after they escaped.

Rob's parents scheduled a family emergency practice drill. Katy pretended her clothes were on fire. She dropped to the ground, covered her face with her hands, and rolled over on the ground.

Rob wrote down and rehearsed what he would tell the dispatcher on the phone. He then pretended to make the emergency 911 call to get help for Katy.

Next, Rob and his family pretended there was smoke in their house. They practiced crawling on their hands and knees and keeping their head about 12 inches above the floor until each of them got to the nearest outside door. Since smoke is poisonous and rises to the ceiling, crawling and breathing the air closest to the floor is safer. After Rob, Katy, and their parents escaped, they met outside at their meeting place. Rob's father pretended to call 911 and report the fire.

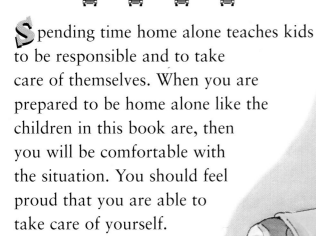

Spending time home alone teaches kids to be responsible and to take care of themselves. When you are prepared to be home alone like the children in this book are, then you will be comfortable with the situation. You should feel proud that you are able to take care of yourself.

Index